FRONT LINES

FRONT LINES

Short stories on
modern society by
writers under 25

edited by
Dan Formby

VALLEY
PRESS

First published 2012 by Valley Press
Woodend, The Crescent, Scarborough, YO11 2PW
www.valleypressuk.com

ISBN: 978 1 908853 10 3
Cat. no. VP0024

Editorial Content, 'Dead Stone' © Dan Formby 2012
'Stop Gap' © Felice Howden 2012
'Viral Marketing' © David Whelan 2012
'This Hopeless War' © James Mcloughlin 2012
'Climb' © Ryan Whittaker 2012
'Patrick' © Nathan Ouriach 2012

All rights reserved. No part of this publication may be
reproduced, stored in or introduced into a retrieval system,
or transmitted in any form, by any means (electronic,
mechanical, photocopying, recording or otherwise) without
prior written permission from the rights holders.

9 8 7 6 5 4 3 2 1

A CIP record for this book is
available from the British Library

Printed and bound in Great Britain by
Imprint Digital, Upton Pyne, Exeter

This book is sold subject to the condition that it shall not,
by way of trade or otherwise, be lent, resold, hired out,
or otherwise circulated without the publisher's prior
consent in any form of binding or cover other than that
in which it is published and without a similar condition,
including this condition, being imposed on the
subsequent purchaser.

www.valleypressuk.com/books/frontlines

CONTENTS

Introduction — 7

'Dead Stone', Dan Formby — 9
'Stop Gap', Felice Howden — 17
'Viral Marketing', David Whelan — 25
'This Hopeless War', James Mcloughlin — 35
'Climb', Ryan Whittaker — 43
'Patrick', Nathan Ouriach — 51

* * *

Front Lines acknowledges the support of NAWE's
Enabling Fund. NAWE (National Association of
Writers in Education) supports young writers
through the Young Writers' Hub:

www.nawe.co.uk/young-writers-hub.html

Introduction

The following stories are six young writers' interpretations of 'modern society' and, in a sense, convey their foreboding, their dreams and their apprehension towards the coming years. Some are explicit in their depiction of societal issues, others display a subtler understanding of humanity. All, however, are poignant.

It was decided early in the editing process for *Front Lines* to seek submissions only from a particular, younger generation. Questions of ageism aside, the point of this book's existence is to tell the world how six members of this generation feel about their 'lot' – albeit indirectly, through the medium of fiction. Most decades have a defining counter-culture; be it the Beat movement, the hippie subculture, or the apolitical skinhead movements of the 70s and 80s. In the last twenty years, there have been less representative counter-cultures in youth and a lot more generalised apathy. Counter-culture, subculture, anti-culture – these three terms are at the heart of this collection.

It is said that the younger generation inherit the previous generation's mistakes – in this time, could such a sentence be truer? With civilisation in its current state, it is easy to recall the perils we face on a day-to-day basis – the collapse of the world economy, a rise in apparently 'humanitarian' warfare, reports of systematic genocide from certain troubled continents – it all gets fairly dark pretty quickly. Hopefully, as you read through *Front Lines*, you won't be put off by the somewhat darker nature of some of the stories – it is a necessity based on the subject matter. The tales told in this book delve into some of the more easily ignored parts of human nature; however, these are also some of the most integral parts of the psyche.

When the opportunity to organise this collection came along, I jumped at the chance. It's rare that a writer early in their career gets a book-sized platform for their short stories, let alone six writers at once. When submissions for the collection began to roll in to my inbox, it became harder and harder to choose between them; everyone had something to say, and they all deserved to be heard. The eventual choice of who to include in the collection was based on a feeling of general satisfaction, with the message of each individual story and the beauty of the writing itself. This collection is a statement – this generation has not stopped caring, has not stopped trying and has definitely not given up.

I hope your reading of *Front Lines* is as rewarding as it was for me to be involved in its invention.

Dan Formby, Editor

Dead Stone

Dan Formby

'Death's a fierce meadowlark: but to die having made
Something more equal to centuries
Than muscle and bone, is mostly to shed weakness.
The mountains are dead stone, the people
Admire or hate their stature, their insolent quietness,
The mountains are not softened or troubled
And a few dead men's thoughts have the same temper.'
– from 'Wise Men In Their Bad Hours', by Robinson Jeffers

I heard tell, once, of a man who took himself away from the life that was given to him. He removed himself from the gifts of the prosperous, the fortunate and the well-mannered, and threw himself into a journey of exploration – both of the ground beneath his feet and into the workings of his own mind. He took himself throughout the differing states of the USA, travelling in whatever way he could, until eventually his feet took him to Alaska, where he planned to settle and live off the land. His name was Christopher McCandless, and he is dead. He died of starvation, and was found in an abandoned bus.

He was an idiot.

So am I.

Our idiocy differs in certain ways, however. McCandless believed that he must travel far away to find his place of spiritual and physical trialling – I was happy to stay far closer to home. He also believed that to do so without training or specific knowledge, with nothing but determination, was the best way to begin and move forward with such a great undertaking. I believe, on the other hand, that an undertaking of any form should be preceded by studious coverage of all things that even remotely involve the concept I find myself a part of. That said, both myself and McCandless share one fact about ourselves at this point in time – I am, as some would say, 'up the creek without a paddle'. McCandless was also, once upon a time, up a creek. He had no paddle. He drowned – metaphorically. One is hoping that I shall fare better – literally.

I would not say that the exploration I undertook was much of an adventure. It did not require the traversing of treacherous chasms or unknown lands, but it was exactly what I wanted it to be; a removal of society from my life – or at least, the society that I was a part of and had come to deplore. I am, geographically speaking, fourteen miles away from the place I used to call home – not exactly the largest expanse of ground ever covered by an intrepid explorer, you would agree.

Before my tale is continued any further, I feel I should explain to you my reasoning; why a person would wish to leave the ties that bind them to civilisation. For me, my logic ran on three different, yet parallel, courses.

The first reason I left was because of human relationships. My friends, my family, the inexplicably constant yet heartbreaking set of girlfriends and the general gregariousness of human nature was slowly but surely moulding me into another mouse to run on the treadmill. Life should be treasured, and never taken for granted, yet I found myself being told by all those around me (on a subconscious level at least) that living my life at the whim of another who told me what to do, be it a mother, a manager, a friend or a wife, was simply the way of things. It wasn't, it isn't and it never will be. Not for me.

In tandem, I began to notice the undercurrents of British society, and could not bring myself to adhere to them. A nation in which prosperous men and women complain that their prosperity is not good enough and deserves to be protected – while doing nothing to protect it themselves but complain; a nation where the government churns insipid politicians into power and acts under the pretence that what they do is in the best interests of the people – while discreetly doing nothing but hoarding riches for themselves; a nation in which the media have no dignity, no discretion, and no qualms – where the money earned from a story is worth more than the life that it ruins. In short, a country at the height of vulgarity, while it languishes in the depths of vague memories of humanity; and to add fuel to the fire, all of its people walk with their heads held high, telling everyone else that we should be oh-so-proud of the country we are miraculously born a part of.

Lastly, though, simply because I could. I'd reached a stage in my life where my friends had drifted apart, a love life was, at long last, fictional and my family were too preoccupied with the distractions of daily life to care about my comings and goings. I simply took the coming part out of the equation.

So, there I was. Purposely putting myself in a position where I had nothing; living in squalor, in abandoned houses and under bridges. Every day became a task not just to be comfortable, but to be alive. Yet the looks my mud-covered face attracted from passers-by gave me a far bigger sense of satisfaction than anything else ever could; Da Vinci's emotions on finishing the Mona Lisa held no comparison against mine, as I considered the masterpiece I had created of my life. Until, as I knew it would, somehow, fate brought its claws biting under my skin once more.

To be part of a homeless community is to be a part of an impossibly diverse counter-culture, yet it is a community and a culture all the same. Here, there are no rules, and the simplest way of getting by is to accept that you must do so through any means possible. When I first ventured into the world of homelessness, I brought with me my thickest, warmest coat, and enough money to at least let me eat for a week or two. Both were removed from me, forcefully, by the end of the first night. The first time I sat and begged for money, I began to truly appreciate the disgust the human soul can hold for those that people see as below themselves. The look in their eyes was either open contempt or purposeful ignorance, countered by those who thought giving pennies was enough to satisfy their karma for a lifetime.

After a few days of begging, the police approached me. They asked me my name, and I told them I didn't know. They asked me if I had anywhere to go, and I said I'd rather not go there. They told me I couldn't sleep where I had bedded down for the night – a park bench of some sort, my memory is hazy on the exact details. I complained – surely, for a homeless man, the rules don't apply? 'I simply don't have anywhere else to go.' They told me they don't make the rules. I was hungry, I was tired, and I was debating whether I had made the right decision. I begged them to let me stay, tried to reason with them. They wouldn't let it go, and one roughly tried to pull me up. I pushed him off, but he tried again. I got angry. I punched one of them. My exhaustion was enough to make the punch weak and futile, but it was enough to be arrested, and I spent a night in the cells.

With no fixed address, the next day they decided to let me go with a caution. As I left, one of the officers from the night before winked as we passed in a hallway. It was then I wondered – had they arrested me on purpose? With nowhere else to go, and looking as forlorn as I did, had they taken pity on me? If so, being arrested was truly the most charitable action I have yet received.

After a few weeks, I had learnt much on the subject of survival in urban environments – the kind of cheap foods that would give me the most energy and did not require cooking, the best places to beg, as well as petty thievery and how to spot a good place to sleep.

It was, for lack of a better phrase, going swimmingly. I had settled, and seemed to be honing my skills. My natural, un-drugged demeanour was so different to other homeless people that I seemed to garner much more money than they did.

I should have known, really.

In any walk of life, nobody likes their next-door neighbour to be more successful than they are.

Nobody likes a show-off. Add to that the natural desperation of the homeless in the first place, and there was bound to be friction.

That's how I found myself here.

The fires burn into my eyes, and I still see red when I close my eyelids. The incessant punching I took to my stomach and ribs has led to a strong, constant, aching pain. My arms hang above me, tied to some sort of piping. I had gone to sleep next to a man who had befriended me, and asked if we could share warmth. I woke up to him tapping me on the shoulder, before he punched me in the temple. Then I woke up here. In between the two fires, a man sits in front of me, his head shrouded in the shadows of the night. Despite my answering of his questions, he refuses to let me go.

'Why do you associate with us?' he asked me.

'Because you are better than everyone else,' I answered. He laughed, and ordered a friend of his to punch me. He then spoke again.

'And what makes you say such a thing?' His voice was soft, and calm. No desperation filtered through his vocal chords.

My own was wheezy. 'Life isn't worth living unless you learn to live it,' I said.

'And this is the way you choose? By taking away the money that could be given to others, less fortunate, more deserving, and believing yourself better for it?' He sniggered once more, and nodded to his man. Another punch met my ribs.

'I don't mean to upset anyone, I'm just trying to find myself.' My voice betrayed my emotions; whimpers were beginning to escape my lips.

'No,' he stated. 'You are here because your life was boring. It was hard and it was boring and it was so easy to be different. So easy to rebel. You are the same as them, but you lower yourself to our way of life and consider yourself better than everyone for it. You remove yourself from the comforts of life and smile, because you're so much better than everyone else. You hold yourself in a higher state of grandeur, as if you are more enlightened because you beg and steal for the sake of it, taking from those that need it more, that could have begged or stole in your place. You are pathetic, and we don't like you.' Not a word that came out of his mouth was in anything other than the dulcet tones that seemed to characterise this man's demeanour. He nodded to his man once more, and a barrage of fists met my lower torso.

When he stopped, I could taste blood in my mouth. The pain seemed to have got to a point where it couldn't get any worse, and the endless thuds into my kidneys stopped bringing any more pain than what was already there.

'It's not like that,' I whispered. I wasn't sure if he could hear me. Tears streamed down my face. 'I just didn't want to be like them.' I took a breath and it hurt inside. I persevered. 'Who are you?'

'Don't you see?' He stood up, and took a step closer to me. I still couldn't see his face. 'You don't fit in here. You haven't lost everything. You aren't an alcoholic, a criminal or a drug addict. There's no catch twenty-two, you can always *just go home*. You pretend you're one of us and expect us to treat you like you deserve the little sympathy we get.' He paused – I imagined he was smiling. 'And me? I am, I suppose, a leader. Every culture has a leader, a hierarchy, someone to ask of and answer to. You may call me King. Or Prime Minister. Or President. Or God. I don't care, really. I look out for my own, and they answer to me. But you are an anomaly. So choose.' He stepped forward, and I saw his face. Dark, sunken eyes and thinning hair, his teeth gleaming yellow with the dirt of years. He was smaller than me, but I dared not speak against him.

'What do you want me to do?' I whispered again. Breathing was getting harder.

'It's not what I want you to do. It's what you want to do that matters.'

'I can't go back to life. The way it was. I hated it.'

He stepped so close to me that his mouth was next to my ear. 'Well we don't want you,' he whispered. 'So, I'm sorry, but you shall be doing neither, I suppose.'

He nodded to his man, who punched me once more, then left. I briefly wondered how each nod differed from the others. As the other man left, the leader sat back in his chair.

Now, he seems to regard me, silently. I'm in too much pain to talk and almost blinded by the constant flickering of the fires in the dark. He sighs. I see the shadow of his head shake from side to side. He stands up, turns and walks away.

Stop Gap

Felice Howden

A kid in a green jumpsuit made from that snow-proof material that has the texture of a crisp packet was chasing pigeons across the square. His arms were out and he was growling, but the pigeons weren't actually paying that much attention; just trailing around with their heads dipping like tiny boats as they plucked at the crumbs of a discarded sandwich. His mother called out to him, but the boy kept running circles on the wet cobblestones until the birds moved into lazy flight. His arms dropped as he turned to see Roger watching him; his body shrank inside his coat and he retreated to his mother's hand, but Roger pretended not to see and finished his cigarette. Then he looked at his watch. There were still at least eighteen hours before he had to be anywhere near the airport. The wind and clouds were moving in with the evening, and the city seemed sharp and grey. Roger didn't have a guidebook or know the names of any local attractions, but there was a pub across the road, so he picked up his bags and crossed two sets of traffic lights. The inside was decorated with faces of old authors and moustachioed men who had brewed their own beer at some point in the last century, and it gave off that same pub smell – a mixture between cooked butter, stale alcohol and detergent – that all pubs had. Roger could have been anywhere. He ordered a pint and took a seat near the entrance.

'Hey pal, have you got a cigarette?' A boy in a hooded jumper was standing over him. Roger took one from his pocket and gave it to the kid, who didn't smoke it, just turned it on its end in his hands and stared. He seemed keen, on edge. 'Alright?'

'I guess,' Roger replied.

'You been on holiday or something?' the boy said, looking at his loaded bags. Roger shook his head, then nodded, then shook his head again and finished with 'kind of'.

'Oh yeah? Where did you go to?' the boy asked, sliding into the four-person booth.

'U.S. I'm just on my way home. Got another plane tomorrow,' Roger said, drinking.

'Yeah, cool mate, nice one.' The boy was nodding now and then said: 'Hey, you fancy a beer or two with me? Nobody's about yet.'

He pulled off his hood. His head was shaved. Roger, dreading equally the prospect of another meaningless conversation and another night alone in an unfamiliar town, assented with a nod of his head. Then the kid was talking about some skating he'd done earlier that week at a place and with people Roger had never heard of. Then the kid was calling for another drink saying 'it's never just one or two, is it?' and Roger nodded again. The sun slid behind the clouds and buildings and Roger looked at his watch, then the kid took off his jumper and started talking about a film he'd seen recently where these three guys had tried to hitch across America but were abducted by Neo-Nazis. Roger spilt his beer slightly down his chin and nodded and realised he should have eaten something. The kid kept talking and he kept nodding, drinking, his hands starting to go slightly numb, and he picked at the hair on the backs of his arms. He had a brief moment of clarity when he got back from ordering some peanuts at the bar and realised the table was full of empty glasses, and the boy was slumped towards him, saying something like: 'but I wouldn't care if I never saw him again, you know?' It was dark outside and Roger had little memory of where the last two hours or the contents of his wallet had gone, but judging by his swirling mind they hadn't been traded for any valuable information. His stomach was hot and rolling.

'I can't drink anymore,' he said, and the boy nodded, his eyes wide and dark like twin pebbles under an icy stream, and even though he'd made his share of the empty glasses between them, he seemed clear, strong and vital.

'I know what we'll do. I have this friend who just came back here, sort of like you but he's staying, and anyway they're all round at my mate's house and we can go there no problem. I can help you with the bags, hey,' he said and Roger was too much of something to say no and he had nowhere else to be until the next day, and the kid's eyes were suggesting something deadly that roused a sharp interest in Roger's mind.

So they were out and ploughing into the battering wind; the boy bent double under Roger's pack and Roger weaving across the footpath. And then there was a door, a fierce voice pulling Roger and the kid inside, a smoky room and a huge man in a singlet telling Roger to put his bag down, to have a drink, have another and could he maybe chore him a Rizla? Roger turned. The boy with the pebble eyes was seated on a beanbag talking to a girl in a fur-lined jacket with the hood pulled up. The room was tiny, full, three people perched on an armchair, four more on the floor near the coffee table that seemed the centre of attention, others moving in and out through the squat door like eels, while the low ceiling forced the smoke downwards into their eyes. In the middle of it all, a boy with blonde hair and a jaw that could slice through stone looked right up through the twisting smoke of his cigarette at Roger.

'Sit,' he said. Roger sat on the free cushion on the couch and swayed to the left. 'Where'd you come from?'

He said 'the pub' and the blonde guy smiled and turned his mouth to the girl on his right who was wearing a beanie with earflaps and had big, dark eyes. She looked at his lips, raised her eyebrows as if to say 'is that all?' and squeezed the boy's hand. Roger was suddenly uncomfortable, and he slid from the couch cushions to the floor, next to a boy in a plaid shirt who was wearing huge sunglasses and a shit-eating smile. He was nodding and chewing, hysterical laughter held back only by a fine string in his throat.

'Roger,' Roger said and held out his hand to the guy, who didn't say anything, just kept nodding and smiling and didn't take his hand, so Roger took his hand back and pulled out a cigarette to stop himself from speaking.

'No, but where did you come from,' the blonde said again. His hand was on the girl's thigh now and she was pulling his fingers.

'Oh. Him. I met, we met at the pub. I just got back from the U.S. and you know I have a flight tomorrow again and stopping over, and what's to do here?' Roger said. He was aware he wasn't making any sense and that the girl in the beanie was watching him.

'Yeah, what were you doing in the U.S.? Holiday?' the girl asked.

'Why else do people go to the States? Not holiday, not business, why else?'

The girl looked at him and ploughed her nails through the blonde's hair, and he seemed to shudder like a mirage as the three people on the armchair got into a small tussle over something, throwing their cups to the ground. Coke and vodka pooled on the carpet then sank into a dark stain.

'Hey!' the blonde said and laughed.

'Control them a bit, would you?' the girl said and the blonde just shrugged his whole upper body and lit another cigarette and closed his eyes. There was a strange smell in the room that sat just below the smoke and sugar and spirits – something bitter and synthetic that Roger couldn't place.

'He doesn't care, it's not his house,' the girl said to Roger, as she took the blonde's cigarette but he didn't seem to notice. 'So where are you going next?'

She sat back on the couch and pulled a leg underneath her and her face melted a little, like snow on a cold windshield, and she looked softer as though she gave a fuck but Roger couldn't answer as his stomach was swirling so much, and then the thread in his neighbour's throat snapped and the boy was falling about laughing, his sunglasses going everywhere and his hands useless as mittens against his face.

'Oh come on, boys,' the blonde's eye blinked open. 'Is there any of that left?'

And then Roger noticed the coffee table, the bags, the tense hunger that crept over the room with these words and the shuddering movement, gentle tapping of a card on the table, small shuffles and tender breaths like nursing a flame into life from ashes, and then a continued long look between the blonde and the girl in the beanie that made Roger feel as though he had walked in on his parents fucking. The boy in the sunglasses was grinning now and pushed something toward Roger and he took it, not really knowing what it would do but aware that he was warm, and that something in the girl's face had given him a feeling he hadn't had since before he left for the U.S. The boy with the pebble eyes was back at Roger's side pointing at people and saying names that Roger wouldn't remember and his heart was beating quickly and he was nodding, agreeing with the kid, telling him things, listening desperately, the information flowing too quickly to grasp anything that passed. A guy in a striped polo shirt suddenly stood from the armchair and said 'I would fucking *love to see that!*' and threw his drink at the wall and pieces of glass and coke and vodka rained like diamonds over the room and the girl in the beanie leaned forward to brush the shards from Roger's hair and Roger laughed, splendid.

The big guy was sitting in front of a TV, messing with the channels and trying to find some music, which he eventually did and then stood up and looked at Roger and said 'you hungry mate?' and took him by the arm through a small doorway into the kitchen where two or three fajitas were sitting on a plate near the sink. The big guy threw them in the microwave and said they'd be ready in a minute and Roger told him thanks and he'd been so starving at the pub earlier and was this his house because it was so fucking cool and he was aware of movement behind him and people laughing and talking and he wanted to join in but the big guy was saying something now and Roger was agreeing and they were grasping hands through the smoke and nodding and Roger was telling him about his flight and how he fucking loved this city and he couldn't believe it and the big guy was saying this is my town this is *my* town you should fucking move here and Roger *fucking would* and he was wasn't hungry anymore so he moved back to the doorway between the kitchen and the living room and watched the girl in the beanie sitting on the blonde's lap. She was purring slightly. The boy who had smashed the glass pushed past Roger to the kitchen where he drank a glass of water and then vomited it into the sink, and he looked up, laughing, with eyes like black holes in his head and water running thick down his chin. He took a small white pill, drank back the water and the big guy put his hand on the guy's back as he vomited again into the sink, the clear liquid rushing through gaps between his fingers.

'I can't keep it down I can't keep it down,' he kept saying and the big guy was laughing, scared, telling him to take it easy and drink some water and pushing another small pill into his wide, wet mouth. The microwave finished and Roger stumbled away through a small corridor with peeling walls to search for the toilet. The first door was to a room where cardboard boxes blocked the entrance and behind that he could see a bicycle wheel and a treadmill tipped on its side and it smelled cold and decomposing like the inside of a fridge, but the next door was the bathroom and there were beer cans floating in the bath and Roger tried to piss unsteadily but nothing came out and he was laughing when he got back into the living room. And then someone turned up the TV; a bass beat with waves of static rolling through and the girl in the beanie was up, moving like a snake through the room to take Roger's hand and the blonde boy was lighting three cigarettes and handing them out and Roger could hear the sound of his own heart or maybe it was the bass drum and he was saying something to the girl and she agreed and they laughed and the music between them was so complete Roger couldn't speak and he thought he might cry so he just kept moving, ready for anything.

Then he was sitting again and the blonde's eyes were narrow, watching him, and the boy who had vomited was back saying something in the blonde's ear. The blonde smiled and said 'you're starting to push my buttons' and his voice was cold. But the boy who had vomited was shaking his head and talking urgently at the blonde and the blonde said 'don't fucking talk to me about that shit.' And the boy's mouth kept moving and his eyes kept darting back to the television as he spoke until the blonde stood to his full height and his long, lean arm drew back as his jaw opened and his teeth came together and he snarled, swung, caught the boy in the mouth with his knuckles and the boy's mouth twisted and he shrank to the right, looked back up, his teeth bleeding over his chin now and his eyes big and angry. The blonde boy shuddered from the shoulders and shouted over the music *if you ever fucking talk to me like that again I will break your fucking face you piece of shit cunt* and the girl in the beanie looked at Roger and smiled and mouthed the words *time to go*. A shirtless boy with small, mean eyes and a cigarette hanging from his mouth came out of a room at the back and told them to all fuck off now and he was sick of the sight of them and the blonde grabbed the girl and the girl grabbed Roger and Roger grabbed his bags and they fled through the tiny corridor, down the stairs with the paint peeling off the walls and the smell like a dead animal and into the bracing wind of the street.

The blonde took off at a pace, his long legs striding through the cold and his hand tightly gripping the girl's fingers. Roger ran slightly to keep up. They paused after a block or so and the blonde pushed his fingers through his hair and kept saying 'you saw that right, you saw that, right?' to the girl who nodded but said nothing. The streets were empty and silent after the close noise of the apartment, and the wind had eased off. Roger could see the beginnings of pale blue nudging at the horizon and a low mist clung to the tops of the buildings. He realised with a jolt that they were back in the square where he'd seen the pigeons. He knew his way from here.

'Do you have somewhere to go?' the blonde asked Roger.

Roger looked at him through clear air. He could see blood from the other boy's chin drying on the blonde's knuckles, and the way he was looking at the girl in the beanie. Roger's heart was slowing and his eyes were starting to remake the jigsaw of the scene.

'Yes,' he said and shouldered his bags.

'Seeya,' the girl in the beanie said and the blonde boy nodded, half smiling, half sneering, still pushing his left hand through his hair as they turned away.

The cobblestones were gleaming from a recent rain. Roger sat and watched the mist shift in the changing light, and lit a cigarette as the sun broke through the spaces between the buildings and pigeons started their descent, breaking the early silence with the sound of wings.

Viral Marketing

David Whelan

'It's funny how the world can be changed by an idea. We imagine the transfer of the product, from out of the dusty room it lives in now, into the owner's soft pink hands, wrapped in blue rubber gloves to preserve the quality of the product, and then into a box cushioned by Air Cap, then into a car, then train, then plane, then train and car again. We imagine how our life will change during the time the package takes to arrive. We wonder whether we will still want one, when we finally have one to call our own – we fear that, maybe, tragically, as soon as we have it in our hands we will feel none of the excitement and anticipation that fuels us now but, rather, look down at the small brass object in our hands and, with a sigh, put it aside on our desk to collect another skin of dust. We start our own bidding page, and remember this whole stupid affair as anything but an intrigued fascination buried beneath a time-released apathy of consumption and disdain. But still, even then, I just think, 'I want, I want, I want.' This is a story about the end of a nation. This is a story about loss. This is everything and nothing.'
– Rupert Smyth, 2025, on the Day of Nothing

Charlie sat at his window and looked out into the field, covered in the last of January's snow. Outside, his sister argued with a man that he did not recognise. She pushed him once, then twice. He pushed her back. And he hit her, knocked her to the floor and crawled, like a dog, on top of her. Charlie looked away at that moment, towards the locked door and the television beside it.

When he was younger his mother had taught him how to block out the bad things. He would imagine he was a mute and blind prisoner in a castle, who was really a prince. He had to pretend he was the prisoner or they would come for him and hang him off the sides of the castle turret. His mother told him that as long as he stayed quiet and pretended nothing was happening, nothing really did happen. *It's all in the mind,* she said, *little Charlie, just ignore it and it will go away.* His mother left him and he, eventually, forgot the story. Yet the seed of an idea remained, and spread.

As Charlie grew up, his imagination failed him. His own mind wasn't as powerful, or as consistent, as the television or the internet. He allowed his mind to be imprinted with their messages and ideas. As he got older, Charlie became more and more dependent on his other life, the one behind the TV screen. One game that he found particularly absorbing was about a spy trapped inside Alcatraz.

And so Charlie turned to his television and played the prisoner, to block his sister's cries out.

In the sky, it seemed the sun had begun to set.

It was only 2pm.

*

Rupert Smyth was an average guy. He would turn up at work five minutes early, sit at his desk and play out his job just like any other man would. He would talk to his boss like an acquaintance and sometimes, maybe once a week, crack a joke that would make them both smile, but never laugh. He would talk to the girls in the office and rate himself a hit. He wasn't a hit, though. He didn't do *badly*, but his name was never talked about as much as Jonathon's or Alex's.

Rupert spoke in a homogenous voice. It would be American, or British, and sometimes Chinese. It was occasionally Russian, even though Rupert had never heard a Russian speak, except in the old movies he sometimes watched. He had that twinkle in his eye that suggested he was smart and forward-thinking, but he was neither. That twinkle was just the dizzying reflection of computer screens, mobile phones and satellites, burned onto his cornea in the shape of a windowless white spark. It simply went nowhere.

On this day in question, Rupert had agreed to meet people he had encountered on the Internet. They had bonded during an online bidding war for an item known as a C-Cross. Rupert had never seen one and he had half a mind to believe that his compatriots hadn't either. After hours of screen refreshes, at a rate of 60hz, none of them won the item. It was won by someone who had never written during the bidding process and who didn't make any noises of victory after sealing the item. He simply disappeared back from out behind his screen, with a smirk and a sip from his drink, got up and left Rupert's reality to limp along the same guided path it always had.

The losing bidders decided it was a good idea to meet for a drink. They chose a small pub just off Chancery Lane. It was perfect for their meeting. It was like the red herring they were chasing. It just didn't seem to add up: once someone entered the front door, they would be greeted by a darkened set of stairs that led into a closed bar, and it was only when the drinker crossed the room and walked up a further set of stairs that they reached the real bar.

Rupert, as always, got there first. The next to enter was a woman. She told him her name was Norton and that she wasn't particularly good at conversation.

'*Conversation*?' Rupert asked.

'Yeah – you know, *talking*. I prefer to write. It's hard to say what you mean, but it's easier to write it.'

Rupert thought on that for a moment, his fingers playing with his shirt.

'Well, I do spend most of my time in front of a keyboard. Perhaps I write more than I speak. But, I don't know – I've always just done both.'

'You have longer to think. Don't you ever worry about how stupid some of the things you say are? We can take time when we type, we don't get that anymore.'

She remained silent for a while after that, before Rupert suggested they bought drinks, which they did. The pub was cold and dry, with fake shelves of books and a definite sense that the general public had long since abandoned it. The barman, a young man with pallid skin and the scraggly unkempt face of a recluse, was cordial, if not particularly interested in their company. He spent the majority of his time staring up at a broken LCD television.

Eventually Rupert broke the silence.

'Where do you think the others are?'

'What others?'

Rupert was quiet for a while. Confused and, to be frank, a little scared of this woman who seemed so quiet, so pale and completely detached.

'You know? The other bidders.'

'There weren't any other bidders. They were all me. Sometimes I get so lonely, I like to make other accounts, to simulate life.'

'Like talking to yourself?'

She paused and looked down at her phone, nestled in her hands. The more Rupert looked at the phone in her hands, the more he thought it looked like an egg, clutched inside a claw.

'Listen,' she said. 'What's your number? Can we just do the rest of this conversation in texts?'

Outside, in the sky, the sun was failing.

*

The world stops for few things, but a great sporting occasion is certainly one of them. Sometimes sport is divisive, but often it unites those who wear red and those in blue for ninety minutes of shared competition. The spectacle is engrossing and people flock in their thousands to watch in person, while others sit in bars, together, and watch in unison.

Martin Gibson couldn't get a ticket to the match, so he went down to his local sports bar in Camden. Martin wasn't a particularly popular character in the area. He was a politician. He had featured in lampooned YouTube videos where he would let people into his house and show them his bedroom, his kitchen, his boyfriend. Martin Gibson's sexuality proved to be quite a contentious topic within the borough, with many of his voters feeling cheated when he announced his sexuality *after* he won the local election – but what was worse, what was even more disturbing to the voting population, was that he was a Manchester United (and a British Superiority Movement) supporter.

Martin took a stool by the bar. All the faces were looking up at the various screens around the room. A sea of red and white greeted him. He stood out in royal blue. No one seemed to notice, their eyes fixed together on twenty-two men chasing a ball behind a screen. Martin felt safe, then. Safe in the anonymity that their fixation afforded him.

Martin sat with his face pointed at the luminous screen. His eyes had been weak for years, but he could make out the blurs. He found it hard to make particular sense of the match, it all changed so quickly, but every so often he thought he saw his least favourite player, Xin Wong. Martin, eyes white and drained, feeling a hunger urged up by his disgust, moved his right hand mechanically over the aluminium bar and signalled the bartender for a pot of pickled cockroaches. He was told that the legs were the delicacies, when they were first brought over from Asia. *In better times,* he had said, *we used to say the 'pièce de résistance'.* Martin put three into his mouth at once and savoured the crunch, the slight resistance on his teeth, and that eventual release of insect juices that dripped down his coarse throat.

Martin wiped his mouth and burped. He rubbed his left eye and looked around the bar, at his fellow fans.

Not one was white. *Fuck this,* he thought. *Since when did China take over the damn world?*

A goal by Manchester United broke him from his hiding place. He jumped up in delight, and shouted an old salute he had heard on a documentary from Nazi Germany.

Fifty sets of eyes turned to look at him. Dead, square eyes. Windows to nothing.

Martin, put out and a little scared, turned his face toward the screen. And that's exactly when it happened.

*

Daniel sat on a sun lounger and fingered his way through a glossy magazine. On the front page his own face smiled back at him. The sun was hot, uncomfortably so, but Daniel insisted on lying outside for at least one hour every morning to keep his tan looking natural.

Just beyond the pool and across the veranda lay his latest fling, a Charlotte Myers. She was intent on making Daniel feel guilty for his actions last night so positioned her sun lounger at the furthest possible distance away from him, whilst still receiving the optimum amount of sunlight.

'You're a fucking pig,' she said across the blue water gap.

'Yeah? And you're a damn bitch,' he replied. Daniel then touched the still-fresh graze on his left arm. *You had to give it to her,* he thought. *She keeps her fingernails in the sharpest, sexiest condition.*

'Look,' he said, 'I'm almost sorry about last night. *Almost.* You deserved to be thrown out of that club. You were a mess.'

'Danny, that cunt kept on calling me a... *hooker*. Do you know how that makes me feel? A hooker?'

'Does it make you feel used?'

'Blow me.'

'If I turn on the TV later and see this on E! or online, I'll be pissed, C. I've got a reputation to uphold.'

She snickered.

'You've got a reputation to rebuild, more like.'

'That was just one time, okay? My man sorted it. I'm clear.'

Silence, and then:

'Would it kill you to stick up for me just once? Jesus, that's all I wanted, Danny. A bit of reassurance from my boyf—'

'I'm not your boyfriend, Charlotte.' Daniel sat up and turned to her. 'I'm not your fucking boyfriend, you got that? You're an accessory. My agent said I needed to lay low for a while, act normal, get a girl...'

Daniel had hated Charlotte the moment he set eyes on her. She was just like every other girl he had seen in the Malibu district of Shanghai. She was tall, of course, and beautiful. But, in the world of uncanny valley, she was the archetypal norm. Sometimes Daniel would masturbate over the ugliest women he could find, just to feel different. Often, when he was making love to Charlotte, he would think of his choice favourites – Margaret Thatcher was his current norm. It made him harder and it got it over quicker. Beauty had become boring to him. The only thing that got him going was the disgusting, the repulsive, and the outcast.

His brother was an actor too, and he was married to Charlotte's little sister. This disgusted Daniel, so he tried to make Charlotte permanent. He thought if he could keep her around, his self-repulsion would keep him in line.

He was wrong.

His internet obsession kept him coming back for more and more. He would endlessly browse anonymous forums, sharing photos of old women, fat women, old men, fat men, animals, corpses. The dead bodies freaked Daniel out at first, but when he was assured that they were completely real he felt oddly released. A fear started to form within his stomach – a dark sense of secrecy and delinquency grew inside of him, like a child. For the first time in so long, he felt alive again and, because of this, he knew he could never, would never, tell anyone of his fetishes, of his true life.

But last week he had been caught and so in came Charlotte. Beautiful, wonderful, mind-numbingly boring Charlotte.

'I'm going in. See you later C.'

'Whatever.'

Daniel stopped.

'No. Not whatever. Don't "whatever" me. Jesus, I could have told you that you were going to say that the moment I spoke. You're so fucking stale.'

'God, relax. Take a Xanax. I left some by the sink in the bathroom.'

Even though Daniel resented the remark, he did take the Xanax and shortly found himself drifting on his bed. He hated the moments of release that accompanied the drug's trip. He didn't like feeling out of control. The truth was, he hadn't been in control of his life ever since he had done that first model shoot for a then small-time Chinese modelling agency. It was a quick buck, or that's how he had described it then. He was such a naïve kid. In many ways he was still naïve, but his reflection reminded him daily that he, on the surface at least, was now a man.

How could he have known that his face would cover every inch of China within the week? How could he have predicted that he would be forced to move to Shanghai to further his career? *When Hollywood goes under*, his agent told him, *the best place to be will be China. Screw India. India's got nothing but curry and cows.* So Daniel moved. He picked up his few belongings and took the long plane journey to mainland China. At the very same time, China launched missiles at the United States. Four miles from his hometown.

The war with China had been bubbling under for over ten years. China had slowly begun to get aggravated by America's brutal creep into the Middle East. They saw it as an unworthy fat bully, who needed more space for his ever-expanding waistline, stealing up all the land owned by the smaller kids. At first, China was fine with their expansion – they were doing it as 'a war against terror', then 'a war for democracy' – but as soon as it became obvious it was a war for oil, China stepped in.

When Daniel's plane touched down onto Chinese soil, he couldn't possibly have predicted that he had backed the right side, or indeed any side at all. Yet, after three years the war was still ongoing. In his own way, Daniel fought for his country. He starred in three small-time action movies, a trilogy about an American insurgent who re-founded America on Chinese soil. The Chinese Empire Magazine called it 欢闹的 (Hilarious) and 荒谬 (Absurd). Daniel had no idea it was a surrealist comedy, acting every scene as if for an Oscar. But the days of Oscars were over. As the sun rose over the Shanghai harbour that morning, Daniel felt in his gut that the final days of the Stars and Stripes were being lived out in every passing second.

As he stood at the window that looked out into the harbour, he heard jets overhead and then nothing. The sun, for the briefest of moments, was smuggled from view and all he could sense was the plummeting foreboding of *them* dropping like love letters from the sky.

And then the sky broke into flames to the violent red-white-and-blue rhythm of *The Star-Spangled Banner.*

*

He sat by his desk, on the phone. The call was the most important one of his tenure, his life. It was a successful operation. The bombs had fallen. Barcelona, London, Delhi, Beijing, Nanjing, Shanghai. America had enacted revenge and China had taken notice. Projected casualties: two million. Projected reaction: serious. The man shifted uncomfortably in his seat. The reality of his decision was a burden he would rather not handle. 'Go on,' he pleaded. 'What of the result?' The result. The true objective. Fresh water. 'Have we gained ground toward the site?' They had. Over fifty miles had been reclaimed. They were getting closer. China's forces were stretched; the Special Ops had slipped in virtually undetected. 'Forecast?' Due to rapidly increasing human population and global warming, all surface water will be entirely used up by the end of the year 2025. The Day of Nothing is coming. But if they secure the site, America might live for a bit longer. The President looked at the small glass of water on his desk. He drank it, deep and true. The end was coming, but they had time. The bombs had bought them life.

This Hopeless War

James Mcloughlin

Again, the faces of the jury morphed terribly into evil, waxen masks, and the whole courtroom began to swirl. There was a mocking laughter in the air and a familiar roar of engines. As the gavel came down, thunderously as ever, Malcolm woke up blearily in the sunshine outside the towering menace of Liverpool Crown Court.

Many feet passed before his tired eyes – left to right, right to left, fore to back, back to fore – as he lay there on the pavement, chained to the trunk of the fancy six-ball lamppost outside the court offices.

Malcolm heaved himself to his feet and took stock of things. His signs were still there, though of little use lying face down ten feet away, as they were. He puffed out the breath of a resigned individual and, inwardly grateful to be left alone for one night, began his morning rant at the passers-by. What a great lot of them there were this morning – *must be just before nine*, he thought.

'JUSTICE! JUSTICE FOR THE INNOCENT! MY BROTHER – MY POOR BROTHER. HOW IS JUSTIN SUPPOSED TO LIVE IN THERE?!' he babbled, grabbing the suit shoulders of one unfortunate fellow who wandered by just that little bit too close. The man extracted himself hastily, looking healthily disturbed by Malcolm's deranged demeanour.

'Freak.'

The morning wore on and the people stoically, awkwardly ignored him and his 'drunken tirades' as the newspapers had interpreted them. That was, of course, until they got bored of the novelty and began calls for council action. Some people kindly brought his signs back over to him, as he couldn't reach them; others chucked coins his way in some misguided act of charity. Not long had passed, however, before Malcolm felt sapped of energy by the harsh summer sun and a lack of nourishment. Soon he slumped down against his lamppost and his thoughts turned towards Justin, his younger brother. Convicted, essentially by a media and police campaign, of the manslaughter of a property magnate's son, Justin now festered away in Strangeways, serving out someone else's sentence. He was innocent. This Malcolm knew with all the fervent faith of a sibling – he had been punished because the only other suspect was the dead boy's step-brother and the courts and the press just didn't want that sort of a story. 'Council estate chav held over trainee architect murder' sold far more copies. Why mention Justin's self-started new business, the countless hours he worked in order to support his wife and month-old baby?

Malc had watched, helpless, as the hammer came down through Justin's freedom; listened as the sentence was passed which tore apart his life, and Maxine's, the baby's, the whole family's really. Justin had been such a rock – Malc always felt like the little brother, looking up to Justin as something of a hero, and felt so guilty at having to just stand and stare as they led Justin away, to twenty-three lost years, no parole. It was like a desertion of brotherly duties, in Malc's eyes. He knew Justin wouldn't see it that way, or his wife, or baby Jamie, when he grew up. None of them would ever blame Malc, but his own guilt ate away at him inside, nipping at his life until he had chained himself to this post in an effort to be rid of it.

Sometimes he protested loudly at anyone within earshot. Mostly he lay, despondently, wondering why everyone else seemed to have disappeared – how could they all have given up on Justin? His mother? Justin's wife? They didn't even care. They came by often enough, but never with words of encouragement. He had to fight this hopeless war alone. Of course, it had no profound effect on the public's view of the whole case – he was just known now as the 'courtroom crier' or 'the Crosby killer's companion'. Such sick, baseless assumptions made the simmering fury inside Malc boil over and that was what kept his raging and pleading going for days, even without food or drink, at times.

The police would arrive every now and then, take him away to a cell – perhaps so that the people could get on with their days without disturbance, perhaps for Malc's own safety. More than once he had been beaten by thugs – drunken youths or vengeful vigilantes, he couldn't say – as he lay and slept. These were the lowest times – aching, brutally hungry and bound, in the vast isolation of the indifferent city; this was when Malcolm most regretted the day Justin had been sent down. Despite having no clear goal with his protest, there was no way he could give it up. That meant victory. 'VICTORY FOR THE DARK SIDE!'

His campaign was a lost cause. Somewhere deep down, he knew this and so did the authorities – why else would they let him keep returning here, to unsettle everyone with his dark murmurs of conspiracies and corruption? They knew he was harmless, although a time would soon come when the public's letters of complaint piled too high to ignore, and something *would have to be done* to put an end to this town centre nuisance.

Malc was stirred from his reeling reverie by the looming presence of someone standing over him. Not walking hastily by, head bowed, but standing firmly in his light, looking straight down at him. He looked up but could not make out a face. The figure was silhouetted against the sun and there was no light from the building behind to illuminate its features.

'Whaddayawant?' growled Malcolm, head slumping back to face downwards.

'Why are you doing this?' came the man's reply. Not a harsh query – mere wonder, curiosity.

'They killed my brother – ah, I mean, they killed... no! They said he killed. THEY SAID HE KILLED!'

'Are you on drugs, sir?'

'THEY CAN TRY! I WON'T TAKE 'EM!'

He looked up to find the man scurrying hastily away, more than a little put-out at the ferocity of Malcolm's reply. Just another suit. Malc cursed his own foolishness – if he had just held it together, if he could explain... but it was no use. The words made sense to him, through the fog of injustice; he just couldn't render them into any sort of coherence for others, so he had become a joke, scorched by the burning belief inside and the twisted image out.

He was, by now, near demented with starvation and dehydration. As far as he could tell (which wasn't very well) he hadn't had anything for nearly three days. More and more often, the scene in front of him would swim out of focus, his stomach giving in to crippling hunger cramps. His limbs shook and he curled up on the floor, coiled around the lamppost, shutting out the light as best he could with his shabby cardboard picket sign. Wishing the entire hateful, corrupt world to end, he blacked out of consciousness. The day wore on and the people wondered at this caricature, this cartoon version of righteousness and protest. They just couldn't delve that deeply into the spurs of activism to understand. None of them had ever veered so far from of the path of normality and had, therefore, no reference point with which to sympathise. They just thought him a nutter, a nuisance – once a novelty, now very much a tiresome fixture of the town.

The days wore on – on the second day after the man in the suit, some track-suited lads took Malcolm's signs, whacking him over the head with them until he grabbed one of them, dragging him around until they began to fear him, unhinged as he looked. They ran away, startled. This was the only notable feature of the next few days. The police seemed to have forgotten him now – no one came to ask him to give up 'this hopeless war on justice' anymore, no council men with clipboards, no journalists with microphones. There was, of course, the odd jeering group with cameras, but, by-and-large, they'd lost interest. Malc was now at the mercy of his own estrangement from society. Yet he couldn't just give up. He couldn't let his brother be treated so unfairly. Illegally.

One day, many days after the signs had been stolen, when his body had almost shut down – he could barely talk for babble, only having survived so far through the occasional bottle of water passed his way by pitying strangers – Maxine paid him a visit. She had Jamie in the pram with her, and looked down on the wasted, filthy figure huddled on the floor with a mixture of horror and pity.

'Malcolm,' she whispered. 'Malcolm, it's me.'

He looked up, with a monumental effort, his breath a weak rasp. Vaguely he recognised her but could not muster up any sound or gesture to demonstrate this.

She knelt down stiffly, in her tight black suit-dress 'Malcolm, everyone's here for the hearing. It's Justin's appeal.'

Malcolm heard all this, but through the fog of dehydration and the ache in his guts, it meant little to him. Appeal?

'We... we didn't know what to do. We tried the council, the police. They just told us... well, you've been so stubborn about the whole thing. And your Mum and me... we've been in Manchester all this time, talking to the lawyers and that. We thought you'd have seen the nonsense in this by now. Why are you still here, killing yourself?'

'J-just...'

'Justin might be getting out – we came to speak to you last

week – do you not remember? You agreed, you said you'd come with us? We tried to collect your signs to take with us, to keep – but you just flipped.'

'Attack! ME?'

'No, no! We were helping. We wanted to get you away from here. Come on, let us get you better. Justin needs you. This isn't helping him!'

'Justin… Just… ice!'

'Jesus Malc! What the hell are you achieving?! We're all over there fighting for Justin, going through all those appeals and stuff, you're not helping anyone! Come on!'

She tried to help him to his feet, but he was a dead weight – he had no will to stand anymore. In his haze, he thought of the smug faces of the councillors, the cops – they knew it would come to this. Let him burn himself out. He can't go on forever. But Malcolm, despite his failing, withered body, still knew. Justin was innocent. Justice needed to be done. He couldn't give up.

Maxine had to leave him. He just pushed out limply, not recognising her anymore. He had broken down completely, crumbled by his own avalanche of righteousness on the hike toward justice. He had taken a treacherous route and it didn't look like he could come back. She pushed the pram towards the courtroom, looking back with a tear in her eye, where Justin's family, Malc's family, stood, ashamed. They had tried to prise him away from his fatal campaign, but the fire in the heart of a madman is the hardest to stifle.

'Perhaps Justin… perhaps… he can h-help?' said his mother with a sob. She had gone from two sons to none in one fell swoop.

Malcolm simply lay there, sliding slowly away from consciousness. In his last few thoughts, images blinked through his mind once more of his brother in the dock, his mother and Maxine collapsing into tears. A great swelling agony in his breast surged through him as he recognised his failure; one final realisation to sap the last of his energy away. There were knives on his skin as the weight of a great futility, added to his severe dehydration and malnourishment, began to shut him down. He lurched forward in that last vision, hands flung out to stop them taking his brother away, but the gavel came down once more between them and all was black.

Climb

Ryan Whittaker

The first time I climbed Everest, I learnt The Lessons. There are three. You haven't got a chance of making it up and down that mountain without knowing them. As soon as your feet sink into snow in Nepal and you take your first breaths outside the plane, you're practicing Lesson One: Acclimatization. You can't climb Everest's height above sea level without acclimatizing. It's the same principle as underwater exploration. You don't pressurize, and then you get air pockets in your blood. Up here, you acclimatize or suffocate.

'How are you feeling?' he asked. His concern was beginning to grate. I told him I was fine, in a stop-asking tone and rubbed the scar on the back of my head. The nylon stitching in my glove caught a scab and I winced. I made a mental note to not do it again.

'Have I ever told you about fungal pathogens?' Randall was the only person I knew who could make me laugh so quickly after he'd annoyed me – but you know that, my love.

'Watch your distance.' I motioned him closer as the rope that bound us at the waist tautened. 'And no, Randall. I don't recall you ever telling me about fungal pathogens.'

'Well, now there hangs a tale.' He smiled and drove his climbing axe into cold earth, squatted down, played with snow. 'There's this fungus that lives in the rainforests. Bugs and things eat it because it gives off this bug's dinner smell.

Once a bug eats the fungus, it starts to lose its will to do this and that. It starts to get other ideas, like, "maybe I'll go *this* way", without knowing where they come from. It's space-fungus, man. The spore gets into the bug's head somehow and takes control of it. It starts riding the little guy around like a Segway with six legs. Eventually, when it has full control, it leads the bug up a tree or tall plant. It wants them to get up there because it wants out of the undergrowth, to get where the light shines. It doesn't end well for the bug. The spore makes it lock its jaw onto something, so it holds still when it's time to burst out of its head—'

'—Is this going to lead into you inferring that we're possessed by Martian Mushrooms?' I dropped my pack next to him, started to set up my tent. 'I'm going to sleep now, if it is.'

Our guide Tsu-ten shouted something from behind me, in Nepalese. Randall said something back that I didn't understand and they laughed together. I suspected it was at my expense. Cold and tired, I was thankful for an escape route from the day. I tried to remember the accident, but those memories were still locked away.

I'd been in a coma. They said I had post-traumatic stress disorder. They said I had amnesia. A mixture of work stress and the accident had burnt me out.

The hospital was what I imagine a nursery would look like if humans were born into adulthood. Every patient there was a helpless, white-gowned 'Why?' machine, ambling around rudderless and asking anyone in earshot their limp questions. When I was there, they let me out into the garden. They let me out because I could still tie my own shoelaces. Your sole purpose when you're that broken is to upset visiting family members by expressing a complete lack of recognition for their faces. 'I don't remember you,' replaces the primal wail for food and heat you'd hear on a maternity ward.

You wake up, with what should be a refreshed, well-rested, straight-off-the-production-line brain. With what's supposed to be pre-loaded with a plug-and-play, ready-for-life attitude – but it's not. It's old clothes. Your mind might as well be a hand-me-down from a stranger. You're wearing a soul that doesn't fit, all baggy and worn in, fished out of the lost and found.

That's how it feels.

You wake up, unlabelled and unsorted thoughts in your head. Thoughts that make you spew words you can't remember learning, let alone know why they're necessary. Your personality is a set of miscellaneous files, mental muscle memory you have no claim to – climbing without ever having learned to climb. You wake up in your hospital bed after the longest sleep of your life, curl up, all elbows and knees, into white cotton covers and ask your wife who she is.

And so she cries. And you have no idea why.

Your wife takes you home, so you feel loved. You feel like someone is missing. Why is he not around? Why has he not visited? So you ask, as if you're scared of forgetting the name again: 'Where's Randall?' And she forgets to smile.

Every time you speak to her is like noticing super-glue seams in a once-valuable antique. You push the question. She tells you that you had an argument with Randall and that you're not on speaking terms anymore. *Too convenient*, you think.

You're in your hallway, that you're told you decorated yourself. It's so alien that it might as well be another planet. A sidelong glance from across your living room; your eyes meet when you look at her. She looks thin. You've been so consumed by getting better that you haven't noticed. Realization dawns that every ashtray in the house is always full, and her makeup is always smudged. When did she last eat? When did she last sleep? She's been smiling through tears and you haven't even noticed.

And she asks you how you're feeling…

Night peeled back at the corners to reveal day and I saw Randall reading at the foot of my sleeping bag.

He read *Hills Like White Elephants* to me, performing both the voices. I sleepily ate my breakfast and Tsu-ten checked our equipment. He had a strange way of only looking at me whenever Randall and I were speaking. I let it slide. Randall told me he liked how Hemingway got his point across. We climbed high, that day.

Lesson Two: You Can't Acclimatize to The Death Zone. They really call it that. Once you get up there, the air you breathe doesn't have enough oxygen content. The higher you go, the less there is. A clock starts ticking and your life is reduced to a pointer on an oxygen tank's gauge, moving left and into the red.

Randall tells me about religion. He tells me that God is in a definable direction.

'All religions have a direction. The older ones, like Tsu-ten's, look to this very mountain. It's their goddess, this mountain. Represents the whole of the universe. We're on holy ground, right now. Every so often they climb to remove the bodies of guys like you and me from the snow. It's so their gods won't be offended; or so they don't trip over us if they decide to come back down the ladders in the sky—'

Up in the clouds, everything means something. The altitude makes every second significant. Time becomes as tangible as snowflakes that you feel hit your skin and melt.

'—I mean... Muslims pray towards Mecca. Christians pray upward; like God is spherical, like the Earth is inside God. The Devil is down. Pan is in nature. Every religion has a direction.'

Night again, and I wondered if dreams could turn black and blue and frost-bitten – we really had climbed high...

Your wife leaves you. Randall calls when she leaves to see how you're feeling. He says he's sorry to hear about her leaving. She left because you told her you'd been speaking to him. She was scared. You told her you'd been speaking to him and all she could do was cry like a baby. You resent her. You hate her. Everything starts to seem better without her because she doesn't want you to learn about your own past. Randall gives straight answers.

Randall tells you that the accident happened on Everest, because you're a climber. You know that already, because every time you see a building you work out the angles. You look for handholds and footholds and use landmarks to judge heights. It feels like wearing your favourite trainers; everything is moulded around you. The tight and pinching feelings of amnesia start to ease in the warmth of open, comfortable, familiar actions. You become a human compass and you're heading inexorably in one direction on feet that are gyroscope steady. You've been reunited with your best friend – you're on a pilgrimage and loving every second of life.

You want to go back to where it started. You want to go back to the mountain. Randall tells you that's the only way you'll ever feel normal again. The only way you'll get your life back...

Morning landed hard. That day, Tsu-ten dropped transmitters into the snow as we climbed.

'What's he doing?' I asked Randall.

'He says we've found some dead climbers. They're planning an expedition soon to bring them down. Those are way-point markers.'

Tsu-ten noticed I was spooked. I think he wanted to take my mind off it.

'He's asking what you do for a living,' said Randall. I told him to say that I was in advertising. Tsu-ten replied. He seemed a little subdued. Randall laughed.

'He thinks you're a shaman,' he shouted, over a tinnitus wind.

'Is your Nepalese malfunctioning?' I asked.

'No. He says you're a shaman, so you're a shaman. Don't argue with the Sherpa, man.'

We trudged on. I tried to work out what Tsu-ten had meant – but then I saw them. So many of them. My awareness shriveled like dead leaves. I wanted to climb out of my own head. Burst out of it into the light…

A harsh and sad voice repeats the words, 'Lesson Two'. And you see a skull with designer gunmetal grey Cebe Checchinel stay-on sunglasses, the model with the gripper headband, nose-pads grafted onto cartilage by subzero temperatures – tissue loss at no extra cost. You see an un-gloved skeletal hand wearing a still-functioning five-hundred-dollar Timex Expedition, heart-rate monitor still flashing at no beats per-minute. You see bones resting inside last year's, luminescent, Helly-Hansen barrier jacket.

You see frost on bone, like brushstrokes, but you can't make out the painting.

You see happy faces, because you can't help but grin once your lips have frozen off. Take some snaps for the family album. Leave the camera on the floor for time-lapse, post first photo into last sleeve and work backwards. Decomposition at thirty-thousand feet, turn it over and turn back time to see the resurrection, just for fun.

And you think, *you stupid bastards, Lesson Two…*

I was pulling on air like an unlit cigarette; chain breathing. Cognition was getting tougher.

Then I saw him and I thought about you, without knowing why.

My inability to grasp the Third Lesson is why you left me. Lesson Three: Don't Ignore Pain. Crucial, if you want to keep your fingers and toes and come back you-shaped.

I looked for Randall's footprints but couldn't find them. There was nobody alive up there but me and Tsu-ten. I heard Randall, he sounded far away.

'You know, the top of Everest is so high that the peak is almost in the stratosphere. There are these things up here called the jet streams. They're like the wind on steroids—'

I saw Randall's long-dead body in front of me. I heard Tsu-ten congratulate me in perfect, unbroken English.

'—the jet streams can flow faster than the speed of sound. Sometimes, when they're up high and the Aurorae Borealis are down low, they mix. Makes the whole sky look like a multi-coloured snow-crash stuck on fast forward; you know, like TV static? You don't get them up on Everest – not this close to the equator. But can you imagine if you did? Can you imagine standing in all that colour? Skin blowing away, becoming part of rivers of pure scintillation – until there's nothing left of you—'

Tsu-ten placed his hand on my shoulder and told me that I'd found him, that he knew I would.

I threw up and fell to my knees. I cried.

Randall is dead. Our *son* has been dead all this time and I didn't know. They said I had post-traumatic stress disorder. They said I had amnesia. I asked you who our son was.

Our worlds, yours and mine, glued themselves back together and the seams disappeared in that moment. And I thought… God – I'm so sorry, my love. I've found Randall and I'm coming home. I know why you were crying, but now I've found our son, and I'm coming home.

Patrick

Nathan Ouriach

With my back against the headboard I can just see out of the window. She is asleep on her side of the bed. The clock in front of me says it is two-thirty in the morning; her digital alarm to my right reads two-twenty. I can see the lightless windows of the houses in the street.

I fold the pillow, place it behind my head and lean back. After an argument I can't sleep like she can. In four hours I will be awake. We will all be awake. In eight hours I will be speaking to eleven year olds about photosynthesis. But right now I am sitting in my bed and looking out of the window, with a strain in my eyes. She never enjoyed sleeping on the wall side. It used to be because she would push up against me in the night and force us both off the bed, the wall next to her lending support. Now it is just habit. I think about waking her up and her speaking me to sleep like she used to. I cough into my fist but she does not move. I try to pull the covers off her but she is gripping the top. *You are definitely far away*, I say quietly. The streetlamps outside shine into our room, and I have to climb over her to get out of the bed. I let the cover fall off me. I place my hands on the windowsill and rest my head against the glass. It feels cold from the condensation. Realizing I am naked I pull her dressing gown around myself. Looking back at the bed I see her asleep. She has rolled over onto my side; the light from the streetlamps shines onto her pregnant stomach.

I sit on the edge of the bed and touch it; her stomach feels different now. I touch it again but this time with more pressure. She rolls over and with a yawn, whispers *dime algo*, or something like that. I look at her but her eyes stay closed. I pull the cover over her stomach and tighten the belt around her dressing gown. I go into the en-suite and turn the light on. The soft humming of the fan exits the bathroom; I leave the door open and hope the noise wakes her. Cupping cold water from the tap with my hands I wet my face and look into the mirror cabinet at a pair of eyes, a nose, a mouth and a cowlick. With my wet hand I try to flatten my hair but it just comes up again. I search in the cabinet for sleeping tablets but I cannot see them. I look in her make-up bag but that is just full of Aldomet and Visken for her high-blood pressure. I look back into the mirror.

We first met at Northampton train station, platform four. She was wearing a red cravat with a matching belt around her waist. I saw her before she saw me. She said *hello* in her broken English and pointed at Euston on a piece of paper she had. Flattening my hair, I smiled and with her biro drew a line from Northampton, wrote down Rugby and then drew an arrow to Euston. She thanked me and touched my arm as we both stepped onto the train. There were two seats free on the carriage and I gestured for her to sit by the window but she insisted on having the aisle seat. We didn't say anything on the train; she was reading a foreign book with a gold and dark-green cover. A baby in front was screaming and I remember her looking at it, rolling her eyes and then looking back down at her book. For three weeks I saw her on platform four. I heard her voice when she spoke on the phone or when she bought her ticket and with her ethereal vowels presumed she was French. It was a night in December when the train back to Northampton was cancelled. It had snowed all day and ruined my leather shoes. I saw her in the platform shelter and offered to take her for a drink somewhere in London. We both drank *Vino de Jerez* at this Spanish bar and she told me about where her brown eyes and her dark, long hair come from. She is from La Mancha; she said it was south of Madrid. She told me about Don Quixote and tilting at windmills and all this stuff about chivalry – all with the charm of her borrowed tongue. Holding my wrists and meeting my eyes, she delicately contorted her tongue, teaching me how to roll my Rs. Refusing to try, I instead finished my drink, making sure to look through the glass at her. I have always remembered her in that light. 'We'll learn together,' she had said. 'It's all about time'. She had told me how in Spain it is important to pour drink into the glass gradually from a great height. 'It is about patience,' she said. On finishing a glass of *Vino de Jerez*, she would always say the same thing: 'tell me something'. We drank *Vino de Jerez* after the first time we slept together. I remember telling her how beautiful her body was. We drank it again in this little café in Santander on our year anniversary; it tasted sweeter there. On moving into our flat I bought two bottles of *Vino de Jerez* and we finished them both whilst sitting on our mattress on the floor. As she poured the remainder of wine into my glass, I realised that no one had ever been as selfless toward me as she had been in that red light. She asked me to tell her something, so I told her all the words I knew in Spanish: sacapuntas, bebé, vivo en Inglaterra and su nombre es Aldonza. She laughed and touched my arm. She got pregnant and I celebrated by having a glass of *Vino de Jerez*. It had an odd taste to it that evening. I thought to myself, it tasted different. She insisted on going sober. It would harm the baby, she would say.

I decide to shave; I will have to do it in the morning anyway. It will make me look younger. I walk out of the en-suite and leave the light on. It might wake her up, I think. Looking back at the bed I see she has dribbled on my pillow. I used to think it was sweet but now it is just her saliva on my pillow. Her eyes are closed and her hair is shorter than it used to be. She had told me it needed to be shorter because there is not always someone around to hold it back for her when she has morning sickness. I didn't have a reply to that. I touch the radiator under the window and it is warm. The birches outside the window are bending left to right. I pick up a pillow I knocked on the floor earlier and hold it to my stomach. It's soft. I think about going back to bed but I am too awake now. I put the pillow on her side of the bed and walk downstairs. It is colder downstairs. On the wall to my left are pictures of our families. She insisted on having a picture of my parents. She always talks about how she misses La Mancha and how she loves her father. There are her parents, sitting on their balcony in the sun, smiling, with their grandchildren. Her father looks as young as me. It must be the olive oil in their diet. There is a picture of my mother and father; they are in a Working Men's Club playing the meat raffle; it was the only one I could find. She says lots of things about family. She says that with a baby coming we need to be patient. I think about my childhood and my father. He was a stonemason and didn't have time for patience. Thirty years in the job and now he can barely walk. We once bonded when I was fifteen, he was off work due to backache and he asked me to wipe deep-heat into his shoulders.

By the front door there is a bag of old clothes that she said don't fit her anymore and need to be thrown out. I can see some things that I have bought her since we've been together. I see the brown scarf I gave her for our six-month anniversary, my old football shirt she used to sleep in and a red belt. Picking the bag up, it feels heavy in my hands. I open the door and the wind touches my naked skin; her dressing gown is too short for my arms. I look for my shoes to step outside in but the closest ones are a pair of her lace pumps. It's only a few yards so I just slip the ball of my feet in with my heels bending the backs. There is frost across the grass. The only noise is the bending birches and the crunch of the hard grass under my lace pumps. Everyone around is asleep. The wind has blown the bin lid open so I throw the clothes bag in from a distance. There is a thud; I think about whether it would have woken her up. I turn and walk back to the house and can see my reflection in the glass of the front door. I pull the dressing gown collar around my neck and step back onto the grass. My heel touches the soil and I can feel the frost. The soil wraps round my feet and I can sense the grass growing around me. My feet are cold and I think about her stomach and my father. We laid new soil in March. The garden looked horrible in the beginning. The neighbour to the right had their orange blossoms and the one on the left had stephanotises at the bottom of their drive. We had soil. She said I was just impatient and that I have to wait for it to grow. To me it was just soil. I look back up at my reflection in the front door and touch my father's nose on my face. *The house is warm*, I think to myself. I go back inside because it is warm.

In the dining room, on the cabinet, behind all the dolls and clothes for the latent baby is a bottle of *Vino de Jerez*. I can't remember how old the bottle must be. The lid is tough and I have to use the sleeve of the dressing gown to force it open. The dishwasher is on and hiding all the glasses so I pick up a mug from the cupboard with hearts on. I wish she were with me and not in bed. I hold the bottle with my right hand and pour the drink from a great height. I watch the liquid fall through the air and splash into the mug, and I pour it until it is just above the brim. I consider the red liquid in the mug. I take my time with the drink and regard the window, watching the snow begin to slowly fall on the garden. My cheeks are still burning from being outside. I put my hand on the radiator and it is cold. On the hob is a baking dish with cold grilled eggplant in tomato vinaigrette. I regret leaving earlier and not eating the dinner she made. Whilst sitting on the bed, before I left, she had brought up the baby again. She wanted to name it after me. I don't know why but we argued about it. Something to do with my name rhyming with 'prick' and it also being my father's name and something else I don't remember. She had put the book of baby names back in her drawer and left the room. I went to the pub and drove for a while. A woman with my mother's voice told me things on the radio. A Spanish CD was the only thing in my glove compartment so I put it into the CD player. In the car I thought of all the things I wanted to tell her. I wanted to tell her how I don't mind naming the baby after me; it's just a name. I wanted to tell her how I don't mind about her stomach getting bigger or her changing her hairstyle or never wearing make-up anymore. I don't mind. I wanted to remind her of all the good things she does for me. The way she rolls to me in the night and holds my arm. Something like that. I wanted to tell her everything. I hummed along to the CD not knowing how much I loved her.

I finish the grilled eggplant in tomato vinaigrette and then clean the dish in the sink. I wasn't even hungry. I let the hot water into the basin and allow my arms to rest in it for a while. The windowsill outside is covered in snow now. I can see the birches begin to withstand the wind. After having dried the dish, I walk back up the stairs, remembering to leave the lace pumps by the front door where she keeps them. The bedroom door is still open so I walk in not making a sound. I touch the radiator and it is still warm. I turn the en-suite light off and close the door. Looking back at the bed I see my future wife carrying my future child. I carefully climb over to my side of the bed. I stroke her hair and she rolls over to my side. I am slightly stuck between her and the wall, but re-position myself. I can see everything out of the window as the sun slowly rises, from our feet to our bodies. Her head is by my side as she touches my arm, *dime algo* she says as her eyes open. I begin to talk.

Dan Formby was born in Southport, 1990, and has recently completed an English and Creative Writing degree at Manchester Metropolitan University.

Felice Howden graduated from the University of Melbourne in 2009 with a degree in English and Philosophy. She promptly relocated to the UK, and now works at a publishing house in central London, living in Oxfordshire. Her short stories have been published in the Australian literary journal *Voiceworks*, and she is a regular columnist for BookMachine.org.

James Mcloughlin was born in Merseyside, 1990, and has a degree in English and Writing from Leeds Trinity University College. His first collection of poetry, *Encore*, was published by Valley Press in 2011.

Nathan Ouriach was born in Northampton, and has a degree from the University of Kent in English and American Literature with Creative Writing. Starting his employment career in a box factory, he progressed to work as a window cleaner, and eventually to placements at the magazines *ShortList* and *GQ*. He is currently studying for an MA.

David Whelan is a journalist and fiction writer based in London. His short fiction has been published by Shortfire Press, *3:AM*, *Gutter*, *Marco Polo Quarterly* and others. He currently blogs about literature, film and TV for *The Huffington Post*. His journalism has appeared in *The Guardian*, *The Times*, *The Independent* and *The Sunday Times*.

Ryan Whittaker has recently completed a degree in Creative Writing at Manchester Metropolitan University. It has been fourteen years since he was last published, the last piece being a poem about a cheetah, written when he was eleven. It ate a rabbit.